WRATH

MARCUS SEDGWICK

Barrington  Stoke

For Peter

First published in 2022 in Great Britain by
Barrington Stoke Ltd
18 Walker Street, Edinburgh, EH3 7LP

www.barringtonstoke.co.uk

Text © 2022 Marcus Sedgwick

A CIP catalogue record for this book is available from the British Library upon request

ISBN: 978-1-80090-089-9

Printed by Hussar Books, Poland

CONTENTS

CHAPTER 1
SPRITES

Thursday, 7 July, 6.30 p.m.

Cassie has now been missing for six hours.

Officially missing that is. It's been six hours since her parents went to the police. The police made a statement asking for information, any information, from *anyone* who might have seen *anything*. But no one really knows how long Cassie was missing before those six hours ... The question isn't as simple as it might seem.

It's Thursday, 7 July. No one has seen Cassie since Wednesday. Everyone just *thought* they knew where she was. Her parents assumed she was at home, upstairs in her room, after she'd come back from rehearsal. So it's hard to say when Cassie really went missing. And I have realised something else: in some ways, she'd already gone missing way, way before all this.

Cassie Cotton. Always a bit different.

You might ask: different from what? Or different from who? And I can only tell you: just *different*. I'm no good at this sort of stuff – describing people, telling stories.

Start at the beginning – that's what everyone tells you. So many people say it. Just start at the beginning of the story. But who knows where the beginning of anything really is?

And with Cassie, there are a thousand places to start, and some of them go back weeks and some go back months. Maybe one place to begin in Cassie's story would be four and a half billion years ago, when the Earth was formed. Or to be precise, a short time after this, when the first atmosphere formed. Because it was then that lightning began to strike, crackling strange red electricity into the space between the heavens and the surface of the Earth.

I told you I'm no good at telling stories.

I'll start about six weeks ago. That was when Cassie told me about the sound.

Only six weeks, but a lot can happen in six weeks. Almost as much as can happen in four and a half billion years. It was during lockdown – the last one, before the start of the summer holidays. The lockdown that seemed to go on for ever, during which we all did nothing, when it seemed the whole world was holding its breath.

No, that's not right. At least, that's not how Cassie thought of it. She believed all the *people* in the world were holding their breath, but the world *itself*? The world itself was breathing.

Breathing, slow and deep.

That's what Cassie told me, and she told me how she knew it was breathing.

She'd heard it.

*

You remember? How strict it was during that lockdown? No going out, no going out for *anything*. Stuck at home, day after day, night after night.

Get up. Breakfast. Schoolwork. Dad would make lunch. More schoolwork for me while Dad phoned places trying to find a job of some kind. Then Dad and I would watch TV. Or maybe I'd practise my drums in the garage till one of the neighbours phoned Dad and he'd tell me I had to stop.

Again.

When I put my drumsticks down, all I'd hear was the silence of a town under lockdown. I could actually hear the silence. It wasn't natural. It was almost spooky.

I would go back into the house. Dad would give me a kiss and mess my hair up, and I'd shove him off.

Then he'd say, "Go to bed, Fitz."

And then, that one night six weeks ago, something different happened: my phone pinged.

It was Cassie.

What are you doing?

Sleeping, I messaged back.

Clearly, Cassie replied. I could imagine that teasing look in her eyes as she thumbed at her phone. Somehow she had this look – I mean, she *has* this look. Cassie can tease you without smiling. She just does it with her eyes. She never smiles. At least, if she does smile, I've never seen it.

Before I could answer, another message came:

Been practising?

I was, I told her, **until the neighbours complained. Again. Surprised you can't hear me from where you are.**

That might have been stretching things. Cassie lives on the other side of the park from us. Her house backs onto it, just like ours does, but it's a big park. And our two sides of the park are *worlds* away from each other. Worlds away.

I'd be happy if I could hear you, Cassie replied. **Anything to drown out that sound.**

What sound? I replied.

That humming. You can't hear it?

What humming? I asked.

Seriously – you can't hear that?

Hear what?! I messaged again.

There was no reply for a few minutes. I thought, *God, I've gone and upset her somehow*. I tried to tell myself not to be so paranoid. Then I wondered why Cassie was messaging me in the middle of the night.

In my mind I imagined walking across the park, in the dark, from my house to hers. We weren't really that far apart, but in lockdown Cassie might as well have been on the far side of the moon.

I wondered if she was only sending messages to *me* late at night or if she was messaging George and Francis too – the other members of our band. Just as I was wondering that, my phone pinged again.

Never mind, said Cassie's message.

I didn't know what to reply and I felt stupid. *Think of something to say*, I told myself. *Why aren't you funnier?* Like George. People like funny people.

Then there was another ping.

I've been talking to the guys, Cassie texted.

So it wasn't just me she'd been messaging. I felt emptier inside.

Cassie messaged again.

Wanna try a new sort of sound?

Sure, I replied. I mean, I'm only the drummer, right? And I had no idea, really, but I wasn't about to say, **No, Cassie, I don't want to try a new sort of sound.**

Neat, she said. **I've been working on some stuff.**

At least someone's made use of lockdown, I replied, which I thought was pretty funny. I waited for a reply, but I didn't get one.

She'd gone.

I turned the light off and lay there in the dark. I tried to hear the sound Cassie had talked about – the humming noise. I couldn't hear anything, apart from that endless silence – if you can hear silence.

I wondered what Cassie had meant by a new sound, and how Francis was going to like that. Francis is in my year at school and he started the band. He made himself lead singer. He named it. *Scott*, he called the band, because his surname is

Scott. It's a terrible name, but no one could come up with anything better. So Francis said anyway.

Francis knew George played a bit of bass, knew I'd got a new drum kit for Christmas. When I say "new" drum kit, I don't mean brand new. I mean new *to me*. It was second-hand of course, but I told Dad I loved it just as much as if it had been brand new, and that was true.

I haven't forgotten Dad's face when he rolled up the garage door that Christmas morning ...

We were both shivering in our dressing gowns in the street looking like idiots. Dad shouted, "Ta-daa! Your new kit!"

His face was all excited, but nervous too, in case I didn't like the present. I could see that, and I was all ready to put on an act and say, *Yeah, Dad, I love it*. But I didn't have to act. It was brilliant.

So about eighteen months ago, Francis came up to me and George one day after school. He said he was forming a band and he needed players. Francis was going to write the lyrics and sing. And he asked if we knew any guitarists.

George said, "There's a girl in S4 who plays guitar. But she's weird. That's what my brother says."

Francis looked thoughtful. "Oh yeah, her name's Cassie something …"

"Cassie Cotton," I said.

George and Francis both looked at me.

"My dad did some work for her parents," I explained, shrugging.

This was true. Dad used to be the manager of a print shop on the high street and Cassie's parents had ordered a load of leaflets to be printed for one of their campaigns. Her parents founded and run a charity called Green Scotland, which raises awareness of local environmental issues – organises protests and stuff like that. They're a big deal around here.

"I'll ask Cassie tomorrow," said Francis, and that was how the band was formed.

So I was lying in bed, wondering what Cassie meant by "a new sound", and how Francis was going to like that. Our band had been playing together for a year or so. A bit more than that maybe, but the lockdowns interrupted it a lot. When school was open, we rehearsed in the music room and I used the school's drum kit, which isn't as good as mine. In fact it's a piece of rubbish, but I couldn't take my drums to school twice a week.

Then I started thinking about Cassie again, and wondered why she'd ended our text conversation so abruptly. There one second, gone the next. No goodbye.

As I lay in bed, there was something I didn't yet know. Because, not long after Cassie heard that sound, she told me that she was going to disappear. And the thing that haunts me is this: I didn't believe her.

CHAPTER 2
PIXIES

Thursday, 7 July, 10.30 p.m.

Cassie has now been officially missing for ten hours. It's half past ten, and I cannot even think about sleeping. I'm lying on my bed, again, staring up at the ceiling, just like I did for hour after hour during lockdown.

My mind drifts. I could roam the whole world in my imagination, go somewhere interesting. I could float up into the sky, miles above the Earth, above a thunderstorm. There I could watch strange white lights sparking and fading. But I don't.

Now that lockdown's over, I could at least be outside. It's summer – the evenings are long.

Dad wouldn't mind. But how can I go anywhere knowing that Cassie is out there somewhere?

At least, I hope she's out there somewhere.

I don't want to think about the alternative. I push the thought away and I remember another night, just like this, a few weeks ago. It was towards the end of lockdown ...

*

Ping! went my phone.

It was late, again, when Cassie messaged me.

Gone eleven, but I wasn't asleep. It'd been very hard to sleep during lockdown. I know I wasn't the only one. I think it was something about the way life suddenly changed, the way the world changed. Our routines got swept away overnight and were replaced with ... with doubt and uncertainty. Every night I lay in bed with my eyes open in the dark, staring at the blackness of the room. I imagined a whole world of people doing the same thing. Thinking about the future. What the future would look like. Stuff like that.

I rolled over in bed when I heard the ping and fished for my phone in the dark.

It's really strong tonight, said the message from Cassie.

I was about to reply, **What is?** And then I pulled myself together, told myself to be a bit sharper – she meant the sound that she'd been talking about.

What do you think it is? I wrote instead, showing her I understood.

I don't know. Come out and listen with me?

You're outside?! I messaged. As soon as I sent it I said to myself, *There, that's the kind of thing I'm talking about – stop being so dumb and predictable. Try to be a bit more interesting.*

So I typed again before she could reply.

Where are you?

In the park, replied Cassie. **Come out. It's crazy.**

Crazy. I must be crazy to go out during lockdown, I said to myself as I got out of bed, and got dressed, and opened the door to my room. I

13

remember kind of watching myself doing all this, yet I did nothing to stop myself.

I crept past Dad's door. It seemed he was one of the few people having no trouble sleeping, despite what was happening in the world. I heard him snoring deeply, even though he'd only just gone to bed. That's my dad.

I remember something Mum once said to Dad – *John, you are such a simple soul.* Maybe that sounds mean, but she didn't mean it to be. She thought it was good to be simple, to be uncomplicated. To be able to sleep deeply every night – something Mum could never do.

It seems I take after my mother.

Crazy, I thought as I pulled on my boots in the kitchen. *This is wrong. This is ... illegal. If I get caught ...* and I couldn't finish that thought, because I didn't know what would happen if I got caught. But I knew it would be bad – for me, for Dad.

I knew no one was supposed to go out. It didn't matter that I wouldn't see anyone, apart from Cassie, and that I could keep two metres away from her. The point is, no one was allowed to do it, because if everyone did it, then the numbers would start rising again. The numbers of sick people. And dying people. So I knew I was being selfish, but I couldn't stop myself.

Where are you exactly? I sent to Cassie.

A second later my phone pinged and I froze, cursing myself for not putting it on silent. I fumbled for the switch and listened for any noise from upstairs.

Nothing.

Dad was still asleep. The whole world was asleep, it seemed, except for me and Cassie, somewhere in the park. I have to admit the thought was wonderful. Thrilling, even.

I unlocked the back door and crossed our tiny back garden. I let myself out through the gate that backs straight onto the park. Then I checked my phone.

Find me, said the message from Cassie.

Oh my god, Cassie.

The park isn't huge, but it's a decent size. And it was almost completely dark. The lights in the park were turned off at night during lockdown – a way to save electricity that

Cassie's parents had campaigned for. There was only a faint glow hanging in the air from the streetlights in town.   No moon, no stars. But at least it was summer, and it was a warm night.

I waited to see if my eyes would adjust to the dark a bit more, then decided they weren't going to. I set off, trying to imagine where Cassie might be.

The park isn't really a park – we just call it that. It's a wide, low hill of grass with three sides. It used to belong to the estate where they built the old hospital. It has an old crumbling wall around two sides of it and a road along the third side. On the other side of the road are the hospital grounds.

This will sound stupid, but it's incredible how different things are in the dark. Even in your own bedroom – the place you probably know best in the world – if you get up in the night and don't put the light on, everything's different. Some parts seem smaller and others bigger. You stub your toe on your desk even though you thought you were far from it. Then you smash into the door, which seems to have moved to meet you.

In the park, it was worse. At first I was filled with a sense of something like excitement. It was the danger of being caught, mixed with the thrill of being out. I hadn't been outside in days, apart from our garden. Dad had been doing the shopping and said there was no point in both of us taking risks. I'd been a prisoner, like we all had, and now I was free. At night. And going to meet Cassie Cotton.

But I soon got lost, even though I grew up here. The park is like a giant back garden for me. As soon as I could cycle, I barely spent any time in the little patch of grass behind our house. That's what Dad tells me. But now I had no idea where I was.

I turned around and around. I thought I saw a faint glimmer of light to my right, but as soon as I looked directly at it, it disappeared. I turned my eyes away slightly and could just see the glow again to the side of my vision. Then I looked at it directly and again it disappeared.

Ping! went my phone.

What's keeping you? Cassie asked.

Nothing much, I replied. **It's just totally black.**

Hang on.

And then the clear twinkle of a phone torch appeared where the faint glow had been before.

I started towards it, texting as I went.

Turn it off before someone sees, I told Cassie.

I saw the light fade to the faintest glimmer and I sped up. I was almost there, but just as I reached Cassie I thought, *Oh! Do I have a mask?* I fumbled in the pocket of my hoodie. There was one in there from the last time I went out, whenever that was.

"I'm here," Cassie said as I pulled the mask on.

It took me a moment to work out where she was, but then she moved and I saw that she was lying on the ground.

Cassie was lying on her front, face down, her arms spread out. Something about it unnerved me. It was like she was holding on to the world. Holding on in case she fell off.

Then Cassie rolled over onto her back, waggling her phone, using its faint light to guide me. I came right up to her and sat down. Two metres away.

In the dark, I could just see the blur of Cassie's bleached white hair and the pale skin of her face and hands.

"You should probably put that away," I said, meaning her phone.

Cassie didn't reply, but she did as I suggested.

"You don't have a mask," I said, and thought to myself, *God, you are about the dullest boy on the planet.*

"Yeah, I'm sorry," Cassie said. "I forgot when I left the house."

I didn't answer.

Then she said, "Listen. Do you hear the humming sound? It's the clearest it's been so far."

I listened.

I listened hard.

It was silent. I really wanted to hear it. But there was nothing.

In fact, I don't think I had ever heard less sound in my life. In the very far distance, I heard a car for a few moments, and then even that was gone. All I could hear was my own breathing.

"Sort of," I said.

"You're lying." Then, before I could answer, Cassie added, "Lie down."

The grass was damp with dew, despite it being summer. But I lay myself down on my back beside Cassie and stared up at the sky. It must have been cloudy, because there were no stars to be seen. I couldn't even see the clouds.

"Listen," Cassie said. "Really try."

"I'm sorry," I said, like it was my fault.

"You really don't hear it?"

"Uh-uh," I replied.

"Well, I guess it's a bit weaker again. It comes and goes."

"What is it?" I asked.

"A hum," Cassie said. "Really low."

"A hum?"

"A hum. Humming. You know."

"What's making it?" I asked.

Cassie didn't reply for a moment, then she said, "I don't know. I think it's coming from the Earth."

"It's in the ground?" I asked.

"No, it's not *in* the ground. It's *of* the ground."

My god, I said to myself, *why are you so slow to understand? Why can't you keep up? Can't you think of something good to say?*

"When did you first hear it?" I asked.

"A few weeks ago," Cassie told me. "When this lockdown started."

"And you hear it all the time?"

"No, I said it comes and goes."

"What do you think it is?" I said.

"You already asked me that."

"Yeah, sort of, I know."

Cassie didn't sound cross with me. She sounded ... very far away. As if she was two miles from me, not two metres.

Then I felt something. She must have been lying closer to me than I thought because I felt her fingertips touching mine, just brushing them. I had a sudden vision of the two of us from far above the Earth, looking down at this park in this town in this country that people call Scotland. Looking at a planet overwhelmed by a virus so small you need a powerful microscope to see it. Two small figures lying on their backs with their arms outstretched and their fingertips just touching.

I didn't move.

I had never touched Cassie before. I had never touched a girl before. I felt an actual physical jolt – a movement of energy. I know it sounds stupid, but I felt it. Our bodies connected slightly in a universe which is composed of nothing but energy, so they say.

I'd forgotten that I'd even asked her a question, but Cassie spoke.

"I think the sound is the Earth breathing," she said.

I said nothing. I wondered if Cassie was losing her mind, and I didn't know what to say, because I liked her so much. Like her, I mean.

No, it wasn't even that. I didn't know what to say because I wanted *her* to like *me*.

"That's why the sound comes and goes," Cassie said. "Over hours. It's like the longest, slowest breath you could ever think of. Because the planet is so big, right?"

"Right," I said. And again I cursed myself.

"Fitz," Cassie said, and I said, "What?"

"Do you ever think about being an only child?"

"Me?" I asked.

Oh my god, will you get with it? I said to myself.

"Yeah, you, Fitz. We're both only children. Do you ever think about it?"

I wondered what to say, not sure why I couldn't just talk to her like I'd talk to Dad – except it was obvious why.

"Well," I began, "I don't really—"

Then Cassie's phone pinged.

She pulled it out, looked at the screen, sat up.

"I gotta go," she said, and stood up.

I got up quickly.

"This was ..." I began.

Cassie wasn't listening – she was looking at her phone again.

She was holding it kind of flat and I could half see the screen, but upside down from where I was standing. I saw the words, upside down, but I couldn't quite put them together in my head.

Suddenly Cassie looked up.

"Fitz, you're standing too close to me," she said. "You know the rules."

I backed off and she waved a hand.

"I'm kidding. Hey, did you hear on the news they might end the lockdown soon? Then we can all get together and make some music again."

That was the moment when I could have asked about getting together with just her, but I simply opened my mouth and then shut it again, afraid.

And Cassie left, trotting away through the darkness towards her home on the expensive side of the park, while I started to make my way back.

I got into bed again, resting my head back on the pillow, and my brain finally assembled the words I'd seen upside down on the screen of Cassie's phone. Somehow it just came to me.

All it said was three words:

Sorry. Come back.

CHAPTER 3
TROLLS

Friday, 8 July, 10.30 a.m.

It's half past ten in the morning on Friday, 8 July. Cassie has been missing now for twenty-two hours. I think about how, somewhere in the upper atmosphere, there are small red bursts of light streaking downwards. The police arrived at half past eight this morning and have just left. They spoke to Dad for ten minutes, then they spoke to me for one hour and fifty minutes. They wanted to know everything I could tell them about Cassie – anything that might give them a clue as to where she's gone.

There were two of them: a man in uniform and one in plain clothes with a grumpy face called Mary. She was the Senior Investigating Officer, she told me, and then she told me to call her Mary, as we sat at the kitchen table. She spoke to me like I was five years old.

"You're James Fitzgerald, correct?" Mary said, looking at a notepad.

"Everyone just calls me Fitz," I said.

"They do?"

There were three boys called James in S1. I ended up being Fitz so everyone could tell us apart. Even Dad calls me Fitz now.

Mary was looking at me as if I was the most boring object in the universe.

"Start at the beginning," she said. Everyone always says that.

"I'm not sure where the beginning is," I said.

Mary frowned, as if I was being awkward, when I was just trying to be honest. I thought that was what you were supposed to do at times like this. Tell the truth.

"Do you have any idea where Cassie might have gone?" said Mary.

I shook my head. "I ... Not really."

Mary sighed. She had put her notepad in front of her on the table. Now she pushed it away and sat back slightly.

"Do you know what the Golden Hour is?" Mary said. I shook my head again, so she told me about it.

The Golden Hour is the first hour after a crime has been committed or, in this case, after someone has gone missing. Information the police get during and about this period is the most important in solving the crime. Or finding the person. And the Golden Hour was already long past, and Mary needed as much information about what Cassie was doing just before she went missing as possible.

Once her lecture was over, I told her all I knew.

We rehearsed on Wednesday night. Here. Dad parked the car in the street so we could use the garage. We finished around ten when Dad said he couldn't stop the angry phone calls from the neighbours any more. Cassie had just packed up and left. Francis and George stayed a tiny bit longer. Cassie's parents say they heard her come in and go straight to bed, but they didn't actually see her. Then, in the morning, she was late coming down for breakfast. At first, they didn't think anything of it because it's the summer holidays. Finally, Cassie's mum went up to find her and she wasn't there. They phoned my dad. Two hours later, her parents called the police.

And Mary kept making me repeat what happened again and again. All I could think was, *Wouldn't it be a good idea to ask* why *she had disappeared?*

So I tried to tell Mary. I tried to tell her about the sound, about Cassie hearing the sound and no one else hearing it.

Mary didn't want to know about the sound. She paused briefly like I was being an awkward child, then we started all over again and went through the whole story once more.

It got to the point where I had tuned out of myself, out of being there, somehow. As I kept retelling the same five or six facts, I was remembering the last time we had rehearsed – before Wednesday I mean.

*

Three weeks ago. Lockdown was over. Leaving just two weeks of school before the summer holidays started. It seemed stupid to me, to lots of people. After all this time working from home, we might as well have finished that way. But the school said we all had to get back to normal as fast as possible and that meant going back into the building and sitting in classrooms.

Normal. Like things were ever going to be *normal*, just the same as before.

No one could focus. Lessons were terrible. The teachers were exhausted. We were a mess too. Everyone was just going through the motions of being at school for the sake of it. No one even had the energy to muck about.

The only good thing was that we could rehearse again.

I got to the music room first, or rather I *thought* I'd got there first because when I opened the door, the room seemed to be empty. Then I came in and saw Cassie lying on the ground with her head inside the bass drum of the kit. It's a kit with no skin on the front of the bass drum, and she was lying on her back with her head and shoulders fully inside it.

"Cassie?" I said. I couldn't see her face, but I knew it was her. I looked at her knees for a moment, bare under her school skirt, then made myself look away. It felt wrong when she didn't know I was doing it.

"Huh?" came her voice.

"What are you doing?" I asked.

"Listening," she said.

She had one hand up in the drum and was flicking the inside of it with her finger. Listening.

"Oh," I said.

"I thought it might be stronger in here," she said.

"You mean the hum?"

Cassie wriggled out and was just sitting there in front of the kit when Francis and George came in.

Francis stopped.

"What's going on?" he asked suspiciously.

"Nothing," said Cassie, and then we rehearsed.

The band had been fun to start with, but it was going weird. I don't think anyone really knew why, but one thing was the music. To put it simply, Francis has appalling taste in music. He just likes the idea of being a lead singer. He's tall and blond and loads of girls fancy him. But I think Francis fancies himself a little bit more than they do.

And he has just *terrible* taste in music. From the start he wanted us to play old rock stuff that even my dad would have found cheesy. And we did our best to push him towards more interesting stuff. So if Francis wanted us to play "Jumping Jack Flash" by the Rolling Stones, we'd try to get him to let us play "Paint It Black" instead. And if he wanted to do a Beatles number, we'd try to make sure it was "Tomorrow Never Knows" or "Helter Skelter" and not "Ticket to Ride" or some crap like that. Cassie was always pushing Francis.

At that last rehearsal, the last one at school, we had just about convinced Francis we should cover "Plug In Baby" by Muse. Then Cassie pulled out her phone and said, "This is where we should be heading."

She hit play and out screamed The Mars Volta with "Cotopaxi". Francis looked like he didn't know what was happening.

"That's music?" he said when it was over.

"No," said Cassie. "That's great music."

"It has a cool time signature," said George, looking at me. "You think you can handle that?"

"Yeah," I said, "sure."

I knew full well I couldn't, but I wasn't going to say that in front of Cassie. I'd just have to figure it out at home in case we ever tried it.

Then, just as we were packing up, a bad thing happened.

Francis said, "Hey, Cassie. Fitz tells us you're hearing things."

Cassie looked at me sharply.

"I didn't," I said. "I mean, I didn't say it like that."

"How *did* you say it?" Cassie asked me.

"I just told them, you know … about the sound you've been hearing."

She stared at me as if I had betrayed her, and I felt awful.

"Can you hear it now?" asked George.

Cassie was silent for a moment. She slowly turned to George and said, "Yep. Can't you?"

George listened. It was quiet in the music room, lunch was nearly over, everything seemed silent.

"There's nothing," said George.

"You're just hearing the heating system," said Francis, looking hard at Cassie.

"So why can I hear it all the time?" Cassie asked. "Everywhere. Any time there's no other sound to block it out."

Francis was sort of sneering. "That why you wear headphones all the time?"

Cassie glared at him, then she just grabbed her guitar case and headed for the door.

"Cassie—" I began, but she ignored me and the door slammed behind her.

"You are such a jerk sometimes," I said to Francis.

"Yeah, well, at least I'm not a jerk *all* the time," Francis said, and stormed off.

"What's he got to be mad about?" I said to George, and George just shrugged.

"You wanna get some chips?" he asked.

The end of the following week was the end of term. We didn't rehearse again. I barely spoke to George, and even less to Francis. I didn't see Cassie, but she stayed in my head the whole time, because ... because I had realised something. Too late, as usual, but I had realised something.

I *had* told Francis and George about the hum. Cassie hadn't told me not to, that it was a secret. But she was upset when I told them.

That meant that she had only shared it *with me*, I realised. It meant Cassie assumed I would know to keep it to myself.

And why was that?

Did it mean what I *wanted* it to mean?

Again I was crushed by the knowledge of how dumb I was. And all this was just a week ago, a week before she vanished.

CHAPTER 4
GHOSTS

**Sometime between Friday, 8
and Saturday, 9 July**

It's late.

It's now a day and a half since Cassie was reported missing. I shouldn't have done it, but I looked some stuff up on the internet about missing people. There was some good news: 99 per cent of young people are found again. I read an article that gave all the statistics. It explained that the reason this 99 per cent seems so surprising to us is that we only hear about the children who aren't found. The 1 per cent. They're the ones who make the headlines and appear on the news. So the chances are really good that Cassie will be found.

But there was less good news too. Of that 99 per cent, 94 per cent are found within 72 hours. That's just three days. After three days, the chances Cassie will be found start to drop dramatically. After a week, you may as well give up hope. And these figures are for all kinds of cases where people go missing. Most kids simply run away from home – and when they get hungry, they come back. But if the reason they went missing is that they have been abducted … there's about a 50 per cent chance that they will ever be seen again.

Another thought I try to push away.

I can't believe that Cassie has been abducted – I don't want to. But there is one thing that worries me. It was something she said when I went to apologise.

*

I had made Cassie's life hell by telling Francis and George about the sound she'd been hearing. Hell at school, I mean. I guessed that Francis had been gossiping about it. There was only a week and a bit of school left after the rehearsal that ended with Cassie storming out. But word spreads fast in school.

Why does one thing catch on and another doesn't? Who knows? But almost everyone was teasing Cassie about the sound, it seemed. The joke was to walk past her, humming. If she saw you and turned to you, you stopped and shrugged. And someone else would start behind her, and the game would begin again.

I didn't see anyone doing this myself, but the whole school was talking about it. George told me that in Cassie's last lesson before term ended, an English lesson, someone started humming. Really quietly so the teacher couldn't hear. Then someone else joined in, a bit louder. And another and then another, till the teacher could hear it, but she couldn't tell who was making the noise. And soon it was the whole class doing it and the teacher couldn't stop them.

Cassie stood up and shouted at everyone. Then *she* got sent to the Head and had to do an hour's detention on the last day of school, while everyone else ran off home to begin their summer holidays.

I knew all this was my fault.

That evening after the last day of school, I sat with Dad with plates on our laps, watching TV.

It's a thing we love to do together. Now that the chippy was open again, he'd bought us fish and chips, which is our treat. Even better, we were watching *The Chase*.

Dad was answering questions like mad. When he gets on a roll like that, I always tell him he should apply to go on the show. I really think he could do it. He might even win some money.

The presenter, Bradley, always asks the contestants, "And what would you do if you won some money tonight?"

They all say, "Go to Las Vegas." Or, "Buy some designer high heels."

And I always wonder if Dad would have the nerve to say, "Make sure we can eat for the next six months, Brad. Times are tough."

I could see Dad wanted me to give him some praise for getting the answers right, to tell him he was doing well, but my mind was elsewhere.

"What's up, kid?" Dad said eventually.

I shrugged. "Dunno."

"Yes, you do. You just don't want to tell me."

"If you're so smart, why don't you go on this show?" I said, and I tried to make it sound funny.

Dad put his plate down on the floor and turned to me.

"It's that girl, isn't it?" he said. "Cassie. Has something happened?"

I shrugged again, then nodded. "Everyone's teasing her, and it's kind of my fault."

"Oh," Dad said. "I see."

He rubbed his chin so the bristles made a scratching sound, then he said, "Are you sure about that?"

"Maybe," I said.

"Maybe. Right. Listen, Fitz ... Did I ever tell you about how your mother and I got together?"

"Only about a million times," I said.

He laughed.

Dad and Mum got together because Dad fell in love with her at first sight. They were both sixteen and at different schools. Dad was working weekends at the cinema, selling tickets and popcorn. And every Saturday Mum would come in with some friends and buy some popcorn and watch a film. And Dad was crazy about her, but she didn't seem to even notice him, even when he smiled when he served her, or made small talk, stuff like that.

And then, one Saturday, in comes Mum to the cinema, not with her friends but with a boy. So Dad told himself off – he realised, why did this boy have the nerve to ask Mum out when he could have done it any weekend for the last year or so? But Dad thought he'd missed his chance – this other boy had beaten him to it. And then, when the film was over, Dad was emptying a bin in the foyer as they walked past and out to a car, and a woman collected them. It turned out that she was their mother, and the boy was Mum's brother. He's my uncle Billy now. Dad didn't know that back then, but he did get the message the universe was sending him, and the next weekend he decided to speak to Mum.

He was all ready to ask her out. But he didn't. When Mum came up to the desk with her friends, to buy her tickets and popcorn, Dad froze. He didn't even smile. She and her friends went in to watch the movie, and it was then that Dad did the Famous Thing.

He walked into the cinema, in the dark, in the middle of the film, and somehow he managed to find her. Dad went over to her, climbing across seats, people shouting at him. And he sat down next to her and asked her out. Dad lost his weekend job because of it, but Mum said yes and they were together for ever. Until ...

It's our family story. Mum might be gone now, but we still tell it from time to time because it's funny. Especially the way Dad tells it, like he was the hero in some romcom.

So all this is just to explain what Dad meant by bringing up the story of him and Mum.

Dad meant, "Have you actually told Cassie you like her?"

And I said, "I guess not."

So the next day, I decided to tell her.

It was Friday – first day of the holidays.

I got to Cassie's house at ten.

I rang the bell and she answered. She looked surprised to see me.

"Don't be mad," I said, but she shook her head.

"What's up, Fitz?" Cassie said.

"I came to say I'm sorry."

She didn't reply to that. She looked ... I don't know, like something was on her mind.

"Can I come in?" I asked, amazed at my bravery.

Cassie's answer was to shut the door.

Then she opened it again, a crack, and said, "Hang on."

Then she shut the door again. I stood there, confused, waiting. Wondering if she was playing a joke on me. Then the door opened again and she came out holding her phone.

"It's a nice day," she said. "Let's go for a walk."

We walked around the park first, skirting the hill. It already seemed an age ago that we had lain in the dark on the grass with our fingertips touching, trying to hear the hum. Cassie was right – it was a nice day, bright and warm. The whole summer was ahead, lockdown over. Things should have been great, but they weren't.

"I'm sorry," I said again.

"You don't have to keep saying that," she said. "I didn't tell you not to tell anyone."

"People can be so mean," I said, and she looked at me sharply.

Then Cassie said the words that have come to haunt me now, the ones I didn't really take seriously at the time.

"Do you ever feel like you just want to disappear?" she said.

"How do you mean?" I asked.

"Like just vanish," she said.

I thought about it.

"Like how?" I asked.

"Like go as far away from anyone on this stupid island as it's possible to get."

"Well, no," I said. "Mum already did that. I don't want to leave Dad on his own."

"Oh god, yes," Cassie said. "I'm sorry."

We were silent for a while, and we walked and walked. Around the park, past the houses and out alongside the river. Then we turned and saw Kinnoull Hill rising up.

"Do you want to go up?" asked Cassie, and I said yes. So we set off up the hill, and with every step I said to myself, *Just say "I like you". It's not so hard; it's just three words: "I like you".* But I didn't. I couldn't.

Then we were on top of the hill, by the cliff, at the bench that overlooks the bend in the river and the fields and the hills beyond. It's right by the top of the drop. There are some bad stories about that cliff, and I don't like it. But I didn't want to say anything about that, so I just said, "Let's go to the viewpoint."

We did. Just a little way back from the cliff edge, past a couple of wind-struck trees, is the real top of the hill. It's called Summit Viewpoint.

There's a semi-circular bench made of wood, with stone for the seat. It's in two halves. One side says, "Think global", and the other side says, "Act local".

"Did your parents have something to do with that?" I asked Cassie, pointing at the words.

"I think so," she said, but her face showed nothing. Someone else might have been proud or something, but there was just ... nothing from Cassie.

She went and stood at this little stone pillar, waist high. The top is a circular brass plaque, with lines pointing out in all directions, showing the names of the hills in the distance.

I came over and saw that Cassie was reading the inscription in the centre.

1948 – Erected by John L. Anderson Esq.
to commemorate Lord Dewar's
munificence in gifting this beautiful
hill to his native city.

"What a right pair of idiots," said Cassie.

"What? Who?" I said.

"These guys – John Anderson and Lord Dewar. Jeez. No one owns the hills!"

"What does 'munificence' mean?" I asked. I could barely say it.

"It means *generosity*. It means this creep John Anderson put up a little *shrine* to say *thank you* to Lord Dewar because he *gave* the hill to the city."

"I guess he owned the land or something," I said.

"Yeah, but what was he doing with it in the first place? He or his ancestors likely stole the land from whoever lived here, and then he 'gives' it back to us. How generous! Arrogance like that makes me really angry."

I saw Cassie's point. We studied Native American beliefs at school last year. I don't remember much of it, but one thing I do remember is how they believe that no one owns the land. You're just looking after it for people yet to be born. I like that idea. I was just trying to put a sentence together in my head about it so I could look less dumb to Cassie, and then she spoke.

"Why have we messed it all up?" she asked.

Cassie went over to the bench and sat down in a flump. I joined her.

"What?" I said.

"The world. Our planet."

"I don't know," I said. "I mean, we do our best. Like we recycle everything. At home, I mean."

"Dad says that's missing the point."

"Yeah?"

"Yeah," Cassie said. "He says recycling is good to do, but it's really just the tip of the iceberg. Dad says people recycle so they feel better about the world. But more so they feel better about themselves. So they feel less guilty. But really the problems are so much deeper than that."

"Yeah?" I said.

"Yeah. Mum tells Dad not to be so pessimistic. You know the charity they run? They're really good at it. I mean, they both made a load of money when they were younger, and then they gave up those *incredibly* well-paid jobs to create Green Scotland. But Mum and Dad don't always agree about stuff. Mum says you have to work with what you've got. And what you've got are people. People who don't understand sometimes, you know, the facts of climate change."

"Who doesn't understand that?"

"You'd be surprised," Cassie said. "Just because we learn about it at school ... Mum says lots of people are just too busy to think about this stuff. Or too scared to think about it. Or too poor. Mum says she feels guilty because she and Dad had made a million before they were thirty, so now they can *afford* to have these jobs that don't pay anything – they can *afford* to be worried about climate change. It's not so easy if you're poor."

I wondered if Cassie was meaning me and Dad, but I didn't really care if she was.

"What does your dad say?" I asked.

"My dad ... You don't want to know."

"Tell me."

Cassie gave a long sigh.

She just looked so unhappy. I wanted to put my arms around her. Not because of the way I

was feeling about her. I just wanted her to be OK.
I had all but forgotten about telling her the way I
felt. *Feel*, I mean.

"What does your dad say?" I asked again,
gently.

Cassie was staring into the distance.
I remember looking at her face in profile. I
remember every tiny detail.

"He says the world has already ended."

"I don't get it," I said. I looked at what Cassie
was looking at: the hills in the distance, the sky
and the clouds. The sun.

"The world has already ended," Cassie
explained. "We just haven't realised it yet."

I looked again at the valley below us, watched
tiny cars crawling along the roads far below, like
insects.

"The world of *people*, he means," I said, and
Cassie nodded.

"Yes. He says the good news, if you can call it
that, is that the planet will go on. There will still
be life. Just not human life."

"But we're still here," I said.

"We are just shadows. We are ghosts waiting to be ghosts. We just don't know we're dead yet. And so on."

"Because climate change has gone too far?"

Cassie nodded.

"Dad says there's a bunch of research that proves we cannot survive now. Not as we are. It says there was a turning point, up to where we could have changed things. Now it's too late – we've passed the turning point."

"And when was that?" I asked.

"I can't remember. Ages ago. Before we were born."

"Jeez," I said. "We weren't even born? How is that fair?"

I was silent for a bit and just stared at the world beneath us.

Then I asked, "What does your mum say about it?"

"Mum says we can't tell people that. I don't know if she believes it or not, but she says we can't tell people. Because if we told people, they'd go crazy. Or do nothing. Or just drive even more cars and fly even more planes and eat even more cows, because what would be the point in stopping?"

Then we both fell silent for a long, long time. It was a warm morning. There was not a breath of wind. I thought that I had never seen my home town look so beautiful, but I didn't feel it. All I felt was pain. And not even mine, but Cassie's.

After a while, I glanced sideways at her and as I did, I felt something slip in my heart.

"You can hear it now, can't you? The hum?"

"Yes," she said. "Can't you?"

I shook my head, and she looked like she might cry.

"But it's so loud right now," Cassie said. "How can you not hear it?"

I shrugged.

"Here," she said, pulling out her phone. "I found this website all about it."

Then she realised she had no reception up here on the hill and put her phone away again.

"I'll message you the website later," Cassie said. "Have a look. I'm not the only crazy one."

We walked off the hill. It was late and we were both hungry. We had sat and talked for a long, long time, and I still hadn't said what I set out to say.

We got back to Cassie's house, coming round by the road to her front door. Her parents' house is huge. There's a drive with a garage with room for about four massive cars, even though they only own one small electric Volkswagen.

At the gate to her front garden, Cassie stopped.

She seemed to be listening for something again.

"Do you want to invite me in?" I asked.

Then I thought I heard something too.

A voice. A shout.

I wasn't sure, but Cassie hurried off to the door, leaving me at the gate.

"Let's rehearse again one day," she said, "soon", and she opened her front door.

As she did so, the sound of shouting came from inside. Two voices, shouting – no, *screaming* at each other. The door shut, with Cassie behind it, and there was the sound of something breaking.

I stared at the door for a moment, then I ran for home like a little kid.

That night, my phone pinged as I lay in bed.

Cassie.

I hadn't dared to text her. I had no idea what to say, and to be honest, I had no idea what was going on.

Here's that website, her message said. **Now tell me I'm not crazy.**

So I stayed up half the night reading the site, and that's what has me worried now.

Because I just looked at it again, and there is something I missed.

CHAPTER 5
THE SCHUMANN RESONANCE

It was a strange website. Not like most websites look, with slick images and nice fonts and stuff. This looked like something older, made when the internet was young – just lots and lots of small plain text, links everywhere, and no design at all.

It was confusing at first, but after a while I found my way to various theories about "the hum", as it was called. I don't really know what I thought of it before, what I thought Cassie meant. But as I read, I started to understand more.

The first thing I found was that up to 1 per cent of people claim to be able to hear it. One per cent of the world is a lot of people, so I wondered why I'd never heard about it before. But the website said that lots of people don't realise what they're hearing until one day they notice it. So they might have thought they were just hearing the fridge humming downstairs in the kitchen, but then one night there's a power cut and they still hear it. And it also said another reason the humming isn't more widely discussed is that people are scared to talk about it because they think they will be called crazy. And I had already seen that happen to Cassie, so I knew that was true.

Then I clicked on a little blue underlined link that said "map", and it opened up a full-page map of the whole world. There were red dots all over it. They were in clumps and patches, but they were everywhere. On every continent, in every land.

You could zoom in, and as I did, the red dots exploded into more red dots. I zoomed in on the UK, and then on Scotland, and the dots just kept multiplying. Then I started to click on individual dots, and text boxes popped up with the story of the sound, submitted by someone living in that place.

"It's like a low noise, like a truck engine in the distance, but all the time."

"I hear this rumbling, humming sound. So low I can barely hear it. It's driving me insane."

"It has to be the Russians. You know they have these secret military bases that emit radio waves. NO ONE KNOWS WHY."

"It's like the sound of a jet, but far away and all the time. But it gets louder and quieter. I don't know why."

"It's like a car engine idling. But there are no cars here – I live in a house in the middle of the forest."

On and on these messages went, and some people reported just what they heard, and others said what they thought it was. And some of their explanations were wild and crazy.

"It's submarine warfare."

"It's made by whales and we hear it through the rocks."

"There are lights sometimes – lights in the sky. It's them. The alien people."

"The planet is angry. It wants us gone."

It was getting late and I was getting tired, and I still didn't know what to make of everything on the website. Then I saw a weird link – the words "Schumann resonance" underlined in blue.

I thought it might have something to do with music. In Music lessons we had studied the German composer Robert Schumann, but when I clicked on the link it turned out to be a different Schumann.

This Schumann was a physicist. He studied the Earth and predicted that there would be low-frequency vibrations in the space between the surface of the Earth and the atmosphere. Schumann said it had to exist because of lightning and other "electrical discharges" in the atmosphere.

I wondered what that meant – I thought lightning was the *only* kind of electrical thing in the atmosphere. Schumann even calculated, mathematically, that the base frequency of the vibration would be 7.83Hz, decades before anyone could actually measure it directly, using scientific instruments to do so. But it turned out years later that Schumann was right.

Anyway, some people said that this is what the hum is – the vibration of the Earth's atmosphere. But then I remembered that Cassie thought the sound was coming from the Earth, that it *was* the Earth, so I wondered if that was wrong. Or if she was wrong. Or if both were right somehow.

I read a bit more about what causes the Schumann resonance – about lightning, and about how lightning isn't the only electrical thing in the atmosphere. I read that there are other things – things with strange names. Sprites, elves, ghosts, trolls, pixies and other names. No one really knows what they are. So, sprites are red flashes of light that occur *above* storm systems. And ghosts are a faint green glow that appears after sprites. It was all really weird and confusing, and I shut my laptop and went to sleep.

*

But I have just been looking at the website again. I don't know why. I just want to understand more about what was in Cassie's head.

So I looked at the home page again, and I saw a link I hadn't seen before.

It said "Regional Investigative Groups". When I clicked on it, I saw a whole list, but my eye was drawn straight away to one that said "Scottish Meet".

I clicked, and there was a white page with a video to play. I was about to play it, then wondered what sound it might make. Dad was asleep next door, and snoring away, but I grabbed my headphones and then hit the play button.

It was a short piece of video, just a couple of minutes. There were a group of guys standing in a forest. It looked like it was dusk – the trees were just dark shadows against the sky, and the people were even harder to make out. Just human forms in a dark forest. And there was this weird droning, humming, whining sound all the time as the camera swung this way and that.

I played it again. And again.

The video was … disturbing, and I wondered if it was what Cassie was hearing. If so, it was no surprise she was acting strangely.

Underneath the video it said: "Sound enhanced digitally to make the hum plain even for those who cannot hear it." I had no idea what that really meant.

And then it said:

> **Scottish Meet.** This video was taken at our last field trip. **Next trip: Saturday, 9 July.** Location is confidential, but if anyone wants to come and participate, email the <u>webmaster</u> for details.

Did Cassie write to the webmaster?

I don't know, but I have to tell the police.

And there's something else I have to do.

I click on the word <u>webmaster</u>, and my email program opens.

I start to write.

CHAPTER 6
ELVES

Saturday, 9 July, 10 a.m.

It's Saturday morning, nearly two days since Cassie went missing. Somewhere high above the surface of the Earth, faint glowing light bursts into life for one millisecond and then disappears.

There is news. But I did something dumb. I was awake all night wondering when I could call the police. When Dad woke up and I told him, he was cross. I mean, I could see he was cross, but he held it in. He just said, "You should have told me straight away, Fitz," but he got me to explain it all again. Then he phoned the number that the police officer had left for us.

I felt so stupid. The moment Dad said it I knew I should have told him straight away. Why do I always think of things too late? I hate that about myself. But I hovered next to Dad as he spoke to someone, then waited, then Mary came on the line. Dad went over it all with her and then he listened.

"Right," Dad said. He told Mary the name of the website.

"Yes," he said, and I was pulling at his sleeve like a little kid. Dad held up his hand to shut me up and then he said, "I see. Oh."

Then he turned to me and put his hand over the receiver.

"Put the telly on," he whispered.

"Dad?" I said.

"Put the telly on!"

Dad turned back to the phone. "Yes, yes. OK. Well, I hope it helps. Bye."

He hung up.

"What am I looking for, Dad?" I said, the remote in my hand, flipping channels.

"Local news."

"But—" I began.

"There! Look, that's it!"

My hand hovered, holding the remote, my thumb about to flip the channel again. Then I saw what Dad was talking about. There was footage from a CCTV camera being played in the top right-hand corner of the local news programme. It showed a black-and-white film of a girl pushing a bike onto a train. I knew at once it was the station in town, and I knew at once it was Cassie. There was no mistaking that bleached hair, which the CCTV had turned into a glowing smear of white on the screen.

A man in the TV studio was talking, and there was text scrolling sideways across the bottom of the picture. They were both saying pretty much the same thing.

"A local 15-year-old girl is missing. Cassandra Cotton, known as Cassie, was last seen in the CCTV footage here, boarding a train to Glasgow yesterday morning."

The CCTV video was on a loop. It was only a few seconds long. Cassie wheels her bike onto the train, through the open sliding doors.

There is no one else in the shot.

Most people still aren't using public transport, even though lockdown is over. Dad says it's like the story about baby elephants. When elephants are small, people who want to use them for tourists to ride on tie the elephant's leg to a sturdy little post. And because the elephant is only small, it can't pull it out of the ground and run away like it wants to. It tries once or twice, but it doesn't have the strength. And the elephant gets so used to not being able to run away, that by the time it grows up and gets really big, it's stopped trying. By now, the elephant could easily rip the post out of the ground, but it hasn't realised that it could. So it stays trapped, a prisoner for these stupid tourists to ride on, for ever. Dad says we've all become like that. The lockdown meant we were confined for so long we have lost the urge to go outside.

"There's something else," said Dad.

"What?" I asked, but I kept staring at Cassie getting on the train, over and over again.

"The police have more recent news they haven't told the TV people yet."

"What is it?"

"They found Cassie's bike," Dad said.

"Where?" I asked.

"On the train. It's been riding the line up and down to Glasgow ever since she got on the 10.43 yesterday morning."

"What?"

"Like I said, up and down, down and up."

"But—" I started to say.

"There's no sign of Cassie. I'm sorry, Fitz."

It didn't make sense. Why would she go to the trouble of putting her bike on the train and then leave it there when she got off? I stared at the TV, which had moved on to some other news item.

"There's something else Mary just told me," said Dad, and there was something in his voice that told me it wasn't good.

"What, Dad?"

"They found Cassie's phone. It was in a rubbish bin on the train. They'd searched it twice, but apparently no one thought to empty out the bins till late last night."

"Why would she throw her phone away?" I said.

Dad shook his head.

"They don't know," he said. "She took out the battery and the sim card, or they'd have been able to trace it, apparently."

He paused, hesitant, letting that sink in. Then he stirred himself.

"Look, I'll put the kettle on," Dad said. "Want something?"

I shook my head.

Dad went into the kitchen and I heard him making noise. All I could think about was Cassie. I was still staring at the TV, not seeing any of it. I pulled out my phone. I'd been checking my emails every five minutes since I wrote to the webmaster last night. Every time I checked – nothing. I hardly ever get any emails anyway, but I had hoped I'd get a reply from the website about the sound. But I'd left it so late to write – the day before the event – that maybe they just wouldn't bother.

I opened my email app and there was still nothing. A completely empty inbox, like normal. And I was just about to put my phone away again when I saw a little "1" in the spam folder. My heart gave two quick thumps and I opened it.

The email was from the webmaster – I saw that straight away.

I clicked on it and read:

We meet at Glasgow Central, under the clock, 12 p.m. Saturday. You'll know us.

Glasgow. The word burned out of the screen at me. Cassie had been on the train to Glasgow yesterday morning. She hadn't been seen since.

I looked at the time on my phone.

It was already 9.10 a.m.

"Dad!" I screamed.

CHAPTER 7
GNOMES

At least the second time I did the right thing. I told Dad what I'd done and he phoned the police station again. He told them about the meeting of the people investigating the sound, and they said they'd be in touch with their colleagues in Glasgow, and ... that was that.

"Look, Fitz," said Dad. "You've done all you can do, and you did well. If Cassie was going to meet those people, then she must have emailed them. They have her phone, so they can look these things up. They'll find her. But you have to understand, the police aren't going to phone us every five minutes to keep us up to speed."

I knew he was right. But it didn't feel right doing anything else but thinking about Cassie, worrying about her.

"Why don't you go out for a walk?" Dad said. "See the boys in the band?"

"No," I said, a bit too abruptly, and Dad noticed.

"Something up?"

"No, nothing. Nothing serious. Anyway, I might go for a walk."

"Good idea. If I hear anything, I'll call you right away. Got it?"

"Thanks, Dad," I said, and I grabbed a coat and headed out of the kitchen door towards the park.

I knew where I was going, and it's where I am now ...

... sitting up at Summit Viewpoint, on one half of that semi-circular bench, where I sat alone with Cassie, talking about the end of the world. Just eight days ago. I'm looking out across the valley and the river and the hills and I'm thinking about all that has happened in those eight days. I'm thinking about brief spikes of light pointing upwards from the top of thunderstorms.

I'm thinking about our last rehearsal, on Wednesday night.

*

There had been some fuss about it, even before the rehearsal itself. The four of us had met on Monday, in Lyall's cafe in town. It felt so weird. The first time I'd been in a cafe or anything like that in months. It was like a totally new experience, something that had once seemed so ordinary that you didn't even think about it. And we sat there and I noticed things. I sat there, and sat there, just noticing things. Sounds stupid, doesn't it? Like, I noticed how noisy the coffee machine was. It was deafening – so loud it was probably illegal. And how people don't look in each other's eyes very much when they talk. Most of the time they're looking elsewhere. I noticed how the letters in the window that say "Lyall's" are backwards when you're inside the cafe, and how the plastic of the "y" is peeling away from the glass.

"But why not?" asked Francis, for about the fourth time.

With school shut for the summer we needed some place to rehearse. And Francis had decided that we could rehearse at Cassie's house. We all knew it was huge. They have a cinema room and something they call "the music room" even though the only one who ever makes music in there is Cassie, jamming on her guitar with her headphones on.

"I said no," said Cassie. She turned her head to look out at the high street.

"I know you said no," said Francis. "I'm asking you a different question. I'm asking you why not …"

"Let it go, Francis," I said.

But he wouldn't. He gets like this sometimes. He has to have his own way.

Cassie didn't answer.

"You have all that space," Francis went on. "There's just you and your folks. You only have to ask them."

"Let it go," I said again.

George said nothing. He was staring at the tabletop, pushing his finger round in spilled sugar.

"George's house is tiny and mine's even smaller," Francis said, which he'd already said about eight times. "And as for Fitz—"

"We can rehearse at mine," I said. Before anyone could say anything else, I went on, "I asked Dad last night."

That was a total lie, and I knew I would have to persuade him somehow. Dad just about lets me drum in the garage until the neighbours go mad, but with the rest of the band too ...

"Dad said he can move the car onto the street while we play," I told them. "So that's sorted. Now can we talk about something else?"

We did, for about five minutes, then Cassie said she was going and that she'd see us at mine for rehearsal on Wednesday.

When Wednesday came round, I was excited. Cassie had said she wanted us to play her new stuff. The new sound. I was nervous too because of the tension we'd had in the cafe, but I'd managed to talk Dad into agreeing to the rehearsal. He said we could have two hours and then he wouldn't be able to stop a full-scale riot, no doubt led by little old Mrs Thrower next door. She's scary.

Dad had moved the car out and I'd been sitting at my drum kit, with the garage door open onto the street. I wasn't really playing, just tapping out rhythms lightly. I was waiting for the others. I was hoping Cassie would be first.

She wasn't.

Francis and George arrived together.

George's dad dropped them off and they lugged in George's huge amp. It has separate channels, so Francis was going to plug his vocal mic into it as well as it being for George's bass. They started setting up and then ... Cassie was late. She turned up after half an hour, on foot. She had just her guitar in a soft case on her back and a bag containing her effects pedals. She was wearing her headphones, as usual.

"Where's your amp?" said George.

"And hello to you too," said Cassie, pulling her headphones down from her ears.

I waved a hand.

She seemed excited, not annoyed at having to walk, or at George's unfriendly greeting.

"Dad was going to bring me," she said, sliding her guitar from its case and setting up her pedals. "Then he couldn't ..."

"But how are you going to ... I mean, what are you—" began Francis, but Cassie interrupted him.

"George's amp has like six channels, right?" Cassie said. "So we'll all play through that. It can handle it."

"It'll sound awful," Francis said.

"We don't have any choice. And anyway, it's going to sound great. Prepare to have your ears expanded ..."

Cassie was acting a little weird. I mean, a little more weird than normal. But she seemed excited too, like I said.

We were about to start when she said, "So, we'll try this new stuff, OK?"

"Sure," I said.

George nodded. Francis didn't say anything, but no one cared.

"Fine, so, George, give me your bass a second," Cassie said.

"What?" asked George.

"Give. Me. Your. Bass," she said. She nearly even smiled, like she had a joke she was about to tell.

"Why?"

"To tune it," she said.

"It is in tune," said George.

"No, it isn't."

"Yes," said George, starting to get mad, "it *is*."

"It's in standard tuning," Cassie said. "It's not in *my* tuning."

"Your what?" asked George, and then Francis just snapped.

"Give her your damn guitar, George."

So he did.

Cassie took it, and then she did the weirdest thing. She started putting it into a new tuning, lowering the top three strings, but all by different amounts. We all watched, speechless.

"Look, George, you just need two basic shapes for what we're gonna do," Cassie told him.

"Shapes?" George said. "You mean chords? I'm going to play chords on a bass?"

"Uh-huh," said Cassie.

"It'll sound awful.'

"That's because guitars aren't tuned right," she said, very calmly, as if she was explaining something very obvious.

"What?" said George. "All the guitars in the world aren't tuned right?"

"Mm-hmm," said Cassie. "Guitars have the tuning they do so you can play all sorts of things, in all sorts of keys. But the guitar doesn't really like it. It's like it's being forced into this one set of tensions, just to make it flexible. But it's not happy. The strings are all unhappy with each other – they're crying out for someone to let them be where they really want to be. See?"

George shook his head and just stared.

So then Cassie showed him these two basic finger positions.

She didn't really play them – she just made sure George understood the shapes and then she gave his guitar back to him.

Cassie slipped her own guitar over her neck. She plugged it into George's amp, into a spare channel. There was the usual loud but short electronic pop and click as she stuck the jack in the socket. I love that sound. It means music is about to happen. Loud music.

"What about your guitar?" I asked.

"It's already done," Cassie said, "but in a different tuning to George's ..."

"Different? Then how is any of—" began George, but Cassie held up a hand.

"Ready? Good. George, you switch between the shapes when I nod. Try a kind of constant strum, up and down, really loose."

George tried it.

I had never heard a bass guitar make a sound like that. It was simply indescribable. A deep, rumbling, resonating roar came out of the amp.

George stared at his guitar, then at the amp, then at Cassie. But he kept playing.

And then she started to play too.

The sound didn't just double in volume, it got three times louder. More. It got *wider* and *weirder*. It was a sound I had never heard before, a constant rolling roar, like a waterfall turned into music. You see, I cannot describe this to you. You cannot describe music. You just have to hear it.

This music felt like something never heard before – if it *was* still music, because I was no longer sure about that. At the same time, it felt like something uncovered from the deep past, from the very beginning of time. I know it sounds crazy, but that's the thought that was in my head.

Cassie had her head down, and then she looked up, smiling at me.

It was too loud to even attempt to speak.

I frowned and pointed at my kit.

She understood what I was asking, and she just smiled and raised her eyebrows, as if to say, "Just go with it."

So I did. I began a drum roll on the floor tom – hard, fast, vibrating. Then I started throwing in mad off-beats, trying to be loose, like Cassie and George were. I began to move the roll around other drums, keeping mostly to the toms, with an odd bright snap on the snare. Somewhere between the surface of the Earth and the ionosphere, spikes of light streak upwards from anvil-shaped thunderclouds.

I was focusing really hard, just trying to go with it. When I next looked up, I saw Cassie nodding at me.

She mouthed something at me: "Yes!"

I saw George looking at me, then he looked at Cassie. They looked at each other, then back at me, and we all just suddenly began to laugh.

Why?

It's hard to explain.

We laughed because of the sound. We laughed at how ridiculous it was. We laughed at how different it was – how new, how free. We laughed from sheer joy. Nothing more, nothing less. It was joy that wells out of you and pours into the energy of the universe.

I was about to stop, but Cassie saw and shook her head.

Now she stepped up to the mic, and she sang.

We had never heard her sing before. And I hadn't thought it would be possible to find a way to sing anything that would go with this insane music we were making, but Cassie had.

Her voice was high, ghostly. It was hard to make out the words, or even if all of the words were even in English, I realised after a while.

Cassie's voice soared down from a high, high place. And with her white hair blazing in the harsh strip light of the garage, it suddenly came into my head that she was an angel.

Then it was over.

There was a brief silence, during which you could hear nothing but the end of the music retreating over the horizon of the Earth, and the low buzz of the amp.

"What the hell was that?" said George, but he was laughing, still staring at his guitar and shaking his head. "Do you have more like that?"

Cassie nodded.

"I love it!" I said. "My god, Cassie, it's …"

I didn't know what to say.

Francis did.

"It's horrible," he said. "You can't be serious."

"Hey," I said. "Don't be rude."

"That's OK," said Cassie. "It's going to take some people a while to get used to it."

Francis was clearly one of those people. He stood with his arms crossed, his face like thunder.

"What am I supposed to do?" he said. "Bang a tambourine?"

"I don't want to sing," said Cassie. "You're the singer. You sing."

"That was singing?" he said.

"Hey, don't be—" I began, but Cassie didn't care.

"Just try it," she said. "Please?"

Francis looked thoughtful for a long time. Then he sighed.

"OK," he said, "but—"

"I don't have the words written down," said Cassie. "You can just improvise. Anything you like. Go with it. I didn't really know how I was going to sing it till I started."

So we did the piece again, and this time Francis sang. It was a mess, but he tried, he really did try. It wasn't terrible, but it also wasn't Cassie.

When it was over, everyone was quiet. I'm not sure why. There was no laughter this time. There was … maybe confusion. Or maybe it was something else, something like wonder. We'd never heard music like this before, if it *was* music. I wasn't sure *anyone* had heard music like that before. It felt like some kind of power. A secret power. And Cassie held the secret.

"Hey, Cassie," I said, after a while of this silence. "That song. Is it a song? Does it have a name?"

"I guess it's a song," she said. "And, yes, it has a name. It's called Wrath."

After a while, we took a break.

Cassie said she needed the loo. I told her to head inside and Dad could show her where it was.

When she was gone, I looked at Francis. I could see he wasn't happy. He was looking like he felt stupid, left out. So I tried to connect with him, get him onside, because I loved this new sound and it was all I wanted to play from now on.

But Francis wasn't listening to me.

He went over to Cassie's bag, where she'd left her phone and headphones.

"Let's see what she's been listening to," Francis said, and he put the headphones on. He hit play without needing to unlock her phone. His face darkened again.

"What the ...?" he said.

He pulled the headphones off and put them on George's head.

Francis started laughing.

"No wonder she's crazy – she's frying her brain," he said. He pulled a face so stupid that George started laughing.

"Here, Fitz, you have to listen to this," Francis said, and handed the headset to me.

I put it on and listened.

It wasn't music.

And it wasn't exactly noise.

It was something even weirder than the sound we had been making five minutes before. There was a lot of noise, white noise, but it felt like it had structure somehow – shape. There were sweeping tones that rolled around a single note. And there was an odd throbbing, beating pulse, all the time, underneath.

I looked up and saw George laughing at the confusion on my face. I saw Francis standing in front of me, daring me to defend what I was listening to, daring me to say it was good.

"She's crazy, isn't she?" said Francis. It wasn't a question. "Crazy girl, huh?"

I could see Francis wanted me to agree. That he needed me to agree. So I did.

"Crazy girl, yeah," I said. But I couldn't make eye contact as I said it, pulling off the headphones. When I looked up, I saw Cassie standing in the doorway of the garage.

She had heard me.

She stood still for a moment, then she picked up her stuff and left without saying a single word.

CHAPTER 8
GIGANTIC JETS

Saturday, 9 July, 11 a.m.

I'm still sitting on Kinnoull Hill, at Summit Viewpoint. I stare at my phone, willing it to ring although I know I have no signal.

From time to time I look out across the wide valley. I see the hills in the distance. It's all very beautiful. It's summer, but this is Scotland and it's one of those summer days that could go different ways. It could tip over into being blazing hot and cloudless, or it could tip another way and the few little white clouds could swell in an hour, skies dark and rain lashing down at the world for hours. It's hard to know the point at which things like this change.

I'm thinking about Cassie. About that rehearsal and about her new sound. About that "song" we played. I want to do it again, so much. I want to make that noise again, *so much* ... It made me so happy. Just for a few short minutes, nothing else mattered. Not Dad, or the virus. Not even Mum. It didn't even matter what I felt about Cassie – how much I liked her, my fear she didn't like me. None of that mattered. The only thing that mattered was that music. I realise that right now it seems like the most important thing in the world is for George and Cassie and me to make the music called "Wrath" again. And I feel bad thinking it, but we don't need Francis to make that sound. That amazing secret sound. That sound full of power that could do ... anything. But now Cassie hates me. And no one has seen her for over two days.

*

"Wrath" it was called. That night after rehearsal, I lay in bed hating myself for being slow yet again, and I thought about the word. Wrath. I've seen it many times in RME – the Bible is full of people's *wrath*. This person has wrath for that person, so-and-so is wrathful with so-and-so.

Meanwhile God is wrathful with *everyone*, which hardly seems fair, since He or She started the whole thing in the first place.

Anger. That's what wrath means. Anger. And I've seen plenty of that recently.

I was angry with myself, because yet again I did what Fitz is so good at doing – I didn't think for myself. I didn't think what Cassie was listening to was crazy. Strange, maybe, but strange is not the same as crazy. If we called everything that's a little new "crazy", there'd never be any progress in the world – that's what Dad says. But I told Francis I thought Cassie was crazy just to make him feel better.

But that was his problem, not mine. He was the one being sulky and mean – he should have been apologising to us. And instead I said something I didn't mean, and Cassie had heard.

Of course I sent Cassie a text later that night, as soon as Francis and George left.

I'm really sorry, I said. **I don't think you're crazy. Francis was being Francis and I am stupid.**

Usually Cassie replied straight away if I texted her. We all got used to that during lockdown – everyone glued to their phone as their only contact with the outside world, everyone's fingers ready to tap out replies, everyone addicted to their devices even more than we'd been before. It's obvious why. And Cassie always replied straight away.

This time she didn't, and I lay in bed that night hating myself, over and over.

Why is it, I asked myself, *you find it so hard to say the things you do believe and so easy to say the things you don't? Will you ever grow up, Fitz? Will you ever be yourself?*

I decided that if Cassie wasn't going to reply, I would go over first thing in the morning, to her house, and apologise in person. I practised what I would say, over and over, and I decided to be honest, to say what I thought. About her, about everything, and from then on I was never going to say something I didn't mean.

In the morning, I was up early, but I made myself wait until nine before going over to Cassie's. So I didn't look desperate, I suppose, but also because I didn't think her parents would want me showing up any earlier than that.

I walked across the park, then down the alley that leads to her street, and made my way up their fancy gravel drive. I knocked on the door.

There was no reply. I waited.

I knocked again, and the second I'd finished, the door flew open.

Cassie's dad was there, glaring at me. His face burning.

"What?" he shouted.

I was so surprised, so shocked, I opened my mouth.

"What the hell do you want?" he yelled at me.

I was terrified. Now the shock had worn off, I was scared that he might hit me.

"I, er, Mr Cotton ..." I began. "I came to see Cassie ..."

"She's still in bed. Now clear off—"

Then someone behind him spoke.

"Oh for god's sake, John, leave the poor boy alone!"

It was Cassie's mum, standing at the back of the hall, her arms folded.

"Don't be such a bully to everyone!" she added, and Cassie's dad turned back towards her.

"That is so typical of you," he screamed at her. "Take everyone else's side but mine, as usual."

He didn't even turn to look back at me as he slammed the door in my face. I heard them screaming at each other as I walked away. I was shaking, but I had other things on my mind.

More anger, more wrath, I thought. *Poor Cassie.*

I remembered that text she'd received in the park the night when we were out lying on the damp grass. **Sorry**, it said. **Come back**. Now I guessed who it was from, and I wondered how often this happened. How often did her parents fight? I wondered about Cassie, the strange girl who wore headphones all the time. Did she do it to listen to something? Or to *not* listen to something?

Anger and wrath were not yet done with me for the day.

I was just at the end of Cassie's drive, at the side of the garage, and turned the corner.

There was Francis, standing, clearly waiting.

I was not pleased to see him, and he was clearly not pleased to see me.

"What are you doing here?" he snarled.

I didn't see why I owed him an explanation, but I wasn't going to bother to hide anything from him either.

"I came to see Cassie," I said. I couldn't help adding, "Obviously."

"What do you want from her?"

"What do I ... what do I *want* ...?" I asked, amazed by his question. "I don't want anything *from* her, Francis. I came to apologise to her."

"Look, this is my band," he said.

"What's it got to do with the band?" I said, and I was getting mad now. The sun was behind him, and he's taller than me, so looking into his face was making me squint. It was like being attacked.

"God, you are so stupid," Francis said, his voice mean, hateful.

I was so mad. I wanted to hurt him. I had no idea what he was on about, but I'd had enough of him.

"Why did you even start a band?" I sneered. "You've got no talent for anything!"

That was stupid, because Francis pounced. With both hands on my chest, he slammed me back into the brick wall of the garage. He'd knocked all the air out of me, and for a moment I couldn't breathe. I realised my head must have banged back into the wall – I felt hot liquid trickling down my neck and I knew I was bleeding from a cut. And all this while Francis breathed, panted, steamed right up close in my face.

"I started this band to get with Cassie," Francis said. "You get it now? I want her."

I was honestly surprised.

"But you didn't even ... you didn't even *know* her ..." I said. "It was George who said she played guitar."

"And you are so naive, Fitzgerald. *Of course* I knew her. I just needed a way to get to her."

To get to her. That was how he put it, and I thought something like this: *Francis, you are a horrible human being, and Cassie will never look at you in a million years.*

At that moment, I suddenly felt calm. The moment had kind of stood still and I had stepped out of it. Seventy kilometres up in the air, gigantic bolts of light appear and disappear in vertical streaks reaching speeds of 50,000 metres a second, turning from blue to red. And I was still slammed up against a brick wall with blood running down my neck and my back. Francis was still an angry ball of hate in my face, but I felt calm.

"Put me down, Francis," I said gently.

"Why should I?"

"Because there are three ladies behind you looking at us and you're making a fool of yourself."

I don't know if Francis thought I was lying, but he let go of me and spun around to see the three old ladies looking at us. They had those little shopping trolleys on wheels – heading for the corner shop, no doubt.

"Everything all right, boys?" said one of the ladies, with real concern in her voice.

Francis said nothing – his anger had transformed into awkward embarrassment. He ran a hand through his hair, while I said, "Yeah, just messing about."

"Are you sure, dear? Oh goodness, are you bleeding?"

I put my hand to my head.

"Just an accident," I said. "It's fine, it's fine."

"You're sure?" said the little lady again.

"Yes, thank you," I said. "Francis is just leaving now."

I looked at him and held his gaze until he looked away first and slunk off down the street.

I ran home, amazed by Francis.

When I got in, Dad saw the blood and he went a little crazy for five minutes. I gave him a story about mucking about on the kids' swings and falling off backwards. I got him to calm down after I let him look at it and see it wasn't so bad after all. Just lots of blood.

"Don't scare me like that," Dad said, and I knew what was coming next, because he says it all the time. "You're all I've got."

But I wasn't thinking about Dad. Or the way Mum left. I wasn't even thinking about being hurt, or about Francis slamming me against a wall.

I was still just thinking about Cassie. That I had hurt her feelings.

What none of us knew then – that morning when I went over and Francis attacked me – was that Cassie was already missing. We *all* thought Cassie was upstairs in her room, right there at home, even as her dad shouted at me for no reason, even as her parents were fighting, even as Francis was taking his anger out on me. But she wasn't at home. She had already left.

And the reason she had left was my fault.

I said that Cassie didn't text back straight away when I'd messaged to say I was sorry, that I didn't think she was crazy, that night after rehearsal, but she did later on.

It's OK, she said, **I don't care about that.**

I'm sorry anyway, I replied. I took a deep breath and typed again: **What do you care about?**

A short pause. Then: **Fitz, do you believe in the hum?**

I thought about my new resolution not to lie – not to myself, or to anyone. Not to say what I don't think, what I don't mean.

I think you can hear it, I messaged.

But do you think it's real?

I hesitated for a long time.

I think it's real for you, I replied.

And I never heard from her again.

*

All of this is running through my mind as I sit on Summit Viewpoint.

I'm wondering which way the weather is headed – if there are going to be storms or fine weather. I'm thinking about the point at which it heads definitely for storms, with no chance of turning back. Of being past the moment where things can be set right. I'm looking at the beautiful gentle landscape, the sky and trees and hills. Of the world. I'm thinking about what Cassie's dad believes, that the world has already ended – we just don't know it yet. And then, without knowing why, I stand.

I feel the need to stand, the desire.

I walk over to the short stone pillar with the circular brass plaque on its flat top – the one that Cassie had laughed at. I remember what she called the two men, those two arrogant men, congratulating each other on *owning* the world.

Then I see it.

It's not much, but it sings out to me at once.

I'm looking at the inscription on the plaque again, and I see something is different.

Someone has painted some of the tiny letters, filled them in, in white, like with Tippex or something.

There are just five letters picked out of the inscription like this, in white. The "w" and "r" of Dewar. The "a" and "t" of beautiful. The "h" of hill.

W – R – A – T – H

On the edge of the plaque, there's a small white arrow made with the same paint. It's pointing roughly north. And now I know where Cassie has gone.

I pull out my phone to check, forgetting that there is no signal up here. I swear and start running for home as fast as I can.

Down Kinnoull Hill, beside the river, into the streets, across the park.

I get a stitch in my side, but I keep running. I am slowing, but I keep running. I burst in through the kitchen door, scaring Dad, who calls after me as I pound my way upstairs. And still I am running, into my room, where I grab my laptop.

Dad appears in the doorway.

"What the hell, Fitz?" he says. "What's going on?"

I can barely breathe, but I'm opening maps, cursing my stupidly slow old laptop as I type. I look up at Dad.

"I know where she is," I say.

"What? Where?"

"There," I reply, and I spin the laptop round.

He comes into the room and crouches down, staring at the screen.

"Where?" he asks again, so I point at the screen, at the place where I know Cassie is – as far away from anyone on this stupid island as it's possible to get, as Cassie herself said.

"Cape Wrath," I say. The very north-west of Scotland. "We did it in Geography last year."

Dad stares at me.

"We have to go," I say. "Now."

He stares at me for a second longer, as around the globe mysterious electrical discharges create the Schumann resonance, and I'm praying ...

Then Dad nods, and I love him.

"Let's go," he says.

CHAPTER 9
BEULAH

It's going to be a long drive, but we just throw ourselves in the car and set off. Dad says we'll get anything we need on the way.

The first thing he does is plug his mobile in to charge and then he hands it to me.

"Start phoning people," he says.

"Who first?" I ask.

"The police. Then Cassie's parents. Then ... I don't know," he says as we pull onto the main road and head north.

Dad has Mary, the policer officer, in his contacts, so I call her. She answers immediately and I explain about the name of the music and about the plaque on Kinnoull Hill. About what

Cassie said about getting as far away as possible. Because that's what Cape Wrath is – the most north-westerly point on the mainland of the United Kingdom.

Mary listens and then says they'll "look into it" and I feel a surge of frustration rise up in me. I tell her to hurry and there's silence at the end of the phone. Mary tells me that they fully believe Cassie is somewhere in or around Glasgow with the hum investigators. She explains that they found an email on her phone, asking for the details of the meeting place, just like the one I sent. The police have every reason to believe she's with those people.

"I don't believe it," I say to Dad as I hang up. "Why take your bike on the train, then leave it? Why put your phone in a bin?"

Dad shakes his head. "But then ... there's the CCTV footage."

"I know, but maybe Cassie got off at the first stop and took another train north instead."

Dad tips his head to one side, more like he's listening than thinking.

"I think you're right," he says. "Will the police send someone ahead of us?"

"Mary didn't say. I guess they will – she just hates admitting I might be right."

"People are like that," Dad says, laughing. "Even police officers it seems. OK, so phone Cassie's parents. The number should still be in my phone."

I call but get an answer phone. I leave a garbled message, trying to explain. Then I just say, "It's complicated. Phone us as soon as you get this."

Dad's wonderful – he's planning, thinking ahead, calm.

"Put the route to Cape Wrath in maps on your phone," he tells me, "and save it offline. We don't know what kind of mobile signal we'll have up there."

"Have you ever been there?" I ask.

He shakes his head.

"Your mum and I talked about it," he says. "It's only five hours away, after all. But we never did. You know, life was busy, and sometimes a place five hours away might as well be the other side of the planet ..."

I try to set a route to Cape Wrath, but the app won't let me.

"I'm not sure there's even a road there," I say, zooming in. I can see some kind of track at least, but the nearest real road is a little to the east in a place called Durness, so I set the route for there.

"We'll figure it out," says Dad, and I hope he's more confident than he sounds.

We've joined the A9 now.

The land is wide and flat, and Scotland rolls by under our tyres rapidly.

"Dad," I say, peering at the dashboard, "you're speeding."

"Let's make good time while we can," he says. "We already told the police what we're doing, right?"

There's hardly anyone else around anyway – the skies are clear and the road is dry. All I can think about is Cassie. In my head there are so many things. I hear everything that we've said in the last few weeks, replaying it all in my mind. I can't shake the idea that I could have stopped this happening if only I had done things differently.

I gaze out of the window at the scenery sliding by and remember lying on the grass in the dark with Cassie during lockdown. I remember our fingers brushing. But above all I have a picture of the last time anyone saw Cassie, on that CCTV image from the train station, her white hair glowing like a streak of electricity. The last image of her is fuzzy, indistinct, and black and white – as if she is already a ghost.

It was late when Dad and I left and the morning is gone. The road sweeps us up into the foothills of the mountains as we skirt the Cairngorms. Then we head back down towards Inverness, where Dad pulls off the road.

"What are you doing?" I say. "We can't stop."

"The car needs petrol," he says. "And I need to pee. And we need to eat. Five minutes and we'll be back on the road."

I go inside the shop while Dad fills the car up, and I put a whole pile of sandwiches and drinks in a basket. Dad comes in and sees the mountain of food I've collected. I see him hesitating. I know what he's thinking: petrol is expensive, petrol-station sandwiches are expensive. And we don't have much money. But then I say, "There'll be three of us to feed on the way home."

He says nothing.

"Won't there?" I say, and I feel my heart sinking as I say it.

Dad looks at me.

"Aye, Fitz, you're right," he says. "Sorry."

We go up to the cash desk. There's an old man working there. He looks like he should have retired years ago. He's skinny as a rake. He looks dry and fragile.

As he adds everything up, he says, "Could go either way."

And Dad says, "Pardon?"

The old man jabs his thumb out of the window.

"The weather," he says, and Dad says nothing but nods politely, because there's not a single cloud in the sky. It's a beautiful day – warm, sunny.

We get back on the road and very soon what the man in the petrol station said looks accurate. From nowhere, clouds start to well up ahead of us. By the time we cross the Cromarty Bridge, the sky ahead looks angry. There's less and less blue sky, more and more blotches of dark grey cloud.

"How long now?" Dad asks, and I check my phone.

"Couple of hours still," I say. Scotland is so big, so empty.

Dad says nothing. I can see he's thinking all sorts of things and I'm not sure that I want to know.

"Wonder what's keeping Cassie's folks from calling us back?" he says.

"Probably too busy screaming at each other," I say without thinking.

"Fitz, that's a mean thing to say. You shouldn't—"

"Dad, they scream at each other *all the time*," I say, cutting him off. So then I tell him all about it. Or what I know, at least. I tell him how I guessed that even during lockdown it was so bad that Cassie ran away, in the middle of the night, by herself, just to get away from it.

I tell Dad how she wears headphones all the time, and how I guessed it was to stop her hearing stuff she didn't want to hear.

And I tell him about the hum – as much as I know.

When I finish, Dad looks thoughtful.

"Poor kid," he says. "Do you think ...?"

"What?" I ask.

"Do you think she can really hear it? Or, you know?"

"What?"

"That all this ... stress ... Her parents, lockdown, listening to weird sounds all the time ..."

"You mean she's crazy," I say.

"No, Fitz, no. Just …"

"What?"

Dad doesn't reply. He doesn't need to. We both know what he's thinking about. He's thinking about Mum. About how, almost without warning, she left. She didn't just leave Dad – she left me too. Because something about her life had been too much for her, and we never really knew what. It had driven Dad crazy for years, trying to figure it out.

"It's not like that," I say to Dad. "She just needed someone to believe her."

"Who? Your mum?"

"No, I mean Cassie. She needed someone to believe her. Just *one person*."

And I don't need to add what I'm thinking: that that someone should have been me.

We drive on. Dad goes as fast as he can on flat open straights, but there are twisty sections too that slow us down. The road takes us past small villages, over open hillsides, through patches of woodland. Then the skies suddenly drop right down above our heads and for five minutes we're hammered with a fierce rain. Just as suddenly we come out of the rain and another five minutes later it's blue sky and sun again.

"Could go either way," says Dad. I know he's thinking of the old guy at the petrol station and, despite everything, we laugh.

The roads are getting smaller. We turn left for Lairg at Bonar Bridge, and the road is hardly wide enough for two cars to pass, with just a faint hint of a fading white line down the middle. As the roads get narrower, our speed drops too.

Then the road improves again, gets wider, and there are straight sections for miles, so we can speed up again.

"My god," says Dad, "it's all so beautiful."

I don't feel like agreeing, but he's right. We pass every type of scenery you can imagine on our route. Mountains, forests, moorland, woods, rivers and lochs, and it's all so beautiful. But all I can think of is what Cassie said her dad thinks about it all: that the world has already ended.

"Suppose it's too late?" I ask Dad, looking at the world.

"We'll find her, Fitz," he replies. "If she's here, we'll find her."

"That's not what I meant," I say.

"Then what—"

"Here!" I say, pointing. "That's the turn!"

And we turn left and join the tiny single-track road that will lead the rest of the way, and Dad never asks me what I meant.

An hour later, with first a long loch to the left, and then another to the right, we eventually pull into Durness.

"Now what?" I ask, looking around.

There's more here than I had imagined there might be.

A pub and hotel. A few shops and lots of signs for local tourist attractions.

Dad points at the nearest shop.

"Let's go and ask," he says.

Five minutes later we're back in the car, heading back the way we came, looking for the Cape Wrath Ferry, with instructions to "ask for Andy".

We have to cross the water. Even though Cape Wrath is on the mainland, the way to it means you have to cross the Kyle of Durness, which isn't very wide, but cuts far inland.

We almost miss the road, one we didn't see as we came up the first time. But now we see it's marked for Cape Wrath pretty clearly.

I don't know what we're expecting the ferry to look like. Not a big boat, obviously, but I thought there'd be ... something. A building at least. There are just a few parked cars at the point at which the road runs out and a slipway enters the water, with a hint of the open sea away to our right.

Somewhere in the world, huge streaks of blue energy are bolting up into the air, far above the lives of people. The Earth is resonating in response, with a deep, rumbling power, and then we see the boat.

It's tiny. Ugly, grey and metal – open, flat but with high sides. It looks like it could hold twenty people at a push. Maybe a bicycle if things are quiet. It has a name painted on the prow, a strange name: *Beulah*. I stare at it for a long time – I don't know why – while Dad approaches the man sitting in the boat.

"Andy?" asks Dad, and the man nods.

He's about Dad's age, I guess, but it's hard to tell. His face is brown and wrinkled. It looks like crumbling rocks, and I guess he spends almost his whole life outside, good weather or bad.

"We need to get to Cape Wrath," I say. "Can you take us?"

Again, Andy nods, like there's all the time in the world.

"Have you seen a girl?" I ask.

Now Andy speaks for the first time.

"She your friend?" he says slowly. "Her with the white hair?"

"Yes!" I cry. "Yes!"

Cassie's here, and I can't quite believe it, but there's no one else it can have been.

Andy frowns. "Then we need to hurry – weather's coming in."

He begins to move, to wave us towards the boat, untying the mooring rope. But he does it as if there is still all the time in the world.

I think to myself, *And maybe there is, maybe there still is.*

CHAPTER 10
WRATH

"Between Heaven and Earth," says Andy, the boatman.

I barely hear him.

We are in the middle of the water. It's not wide, not a long journey at all, a few hundred metres, but I suddenly have a sense that we are nowhere.

Did Cassie really come all the way here by herself?

But Andy has seen her – he says he brought her across the water, earlier today. And she had a head start, so she must have stopped and spent the night somewhere on the way. Is that why she made it look like she'd headed for Glasgow? To buy some time? But what has she come here for? It's the question that's been at the back of my mind ever since I saw those five white letters on the inscription.

"Between Heaven and Earth," says Andy again. I don't understand; I don't take it in. I know this sounds crazy, but I can barely hear anything. There's a ton of noise – the engine of the boat, the slap of water on the hull, the wind rising – but I feel like I'm deaf.

"You were looking at her name," says Andy, and I finally look at him.

"Sorry?" I ask.

"The name of the boat," he says, half a smile on his face. "*Beulah*."

"Oh," I say, "yes."

"Between Heaven and Earth," Andy says. "That's what it means."

"Oh," I say. "Yes. Right."

Dad is sitting nearby. He keeps glancing at Andy, and I know he wants to say something, but he also wants us to get across as fast as possible.

And the little boat chugs on through the waves, which are getting rougher. But now we're sliding up to the slipway on the far side. We've only crossed a short space of water, but I have a weird feeling like we've crossed something much bigger, something much more significant. As if we have landed in a foreign country, another world.

As we get out of the boat, Dad says what's been on his mind. "Andy, do you often ferry unaccompanied children across the Kyle?"

Andy frowns.

"She didn't look like a child to me," he says. "Anyway, it's not my business to decide who comes here – I'm just the ferryman."

Andy holds Dad's eye for a moment, till Dad looks away.

He turns, and we realise we have a problem.

A single rocky track leads up from the slipway and over the brow of a hill. It's clearly the way to Cape Wrath – there are no other roads or even paths.

"Is it far to Cape Wrath?" asks Dad.

I'm looking at my phone, which has one bar of signal and is refusing to load anything. I start to open my photos to look at the screenshots I've taken as Andy replies.

"No, not far," he says slowly. "About eleven miles."

"Listen, this could be an emergency," says Dad, glancing at me as he does. "We have to hurry. Is there some way we can—"

"Aye," says Andy, and nods at a beaten-up old minibus parked nearby. It's in such a state I thought it was a wreck someone had dumped there. "There's the shuttle."

"And is the driver around?" asks Dad.

"You're looking at him," says Andy. He is seriously starting to wind us both up now. But he waves a hand. "Climb aboard – I'll run you there."

Now we're in the minibus, rattling and banging our way across the most desolate landscape I have ever seen. It's the end of the world – it has to be. The sky is lowering over wide open land – boggy ground, drab brown grasses and reeds as far as the eye can see.

Not a single tree or building of any kind. The rough and broken gravel track seems as if it's losing a fight with nature, with grass down the middle, puddles everywhere.

The road isn't even straight – it twists and turns, south, then north again, then west, then north, as if it has no idea how to get to where it's supposed to be taking us.

Andy does not speak.

We do not speak.

Rain starts to hit the windscreen, fat drops that smack the glass, and I look out of the window and see darker and darker clouds coming.

Then, finally, we're there.

The sound of the ocean is the first thing.

We can't yet see it, but as we climb out of the minibus we can hear the powerful roar of the ocean, very close by. We've arrived near a series of low white buildings. There's something that might be a cafe. But everything is dominated by the lighthouse – tall, strong, with a white base and a black section housing the light. It has another small building next to it, and there are broken stone walls running across the land. I can sense we are on high cliffs, and the ocean is somewhere just ahead, booming and howling. Waiting.

Rain smacks our faces, our bare hands.

The sky darkens some more.

For a small place, Cassie could be anywhere.

"We'll split up," says Dad. "Meet here if you find anything."

Anything? I think, but I don't stop to argue. I run.

Dad heads for the cafe and I head for the lighthouse.

I circle the base – there's a door but it's locked, and so are the doors of the low building that sits to the side. The land dips and rolls, and the broken stone wall is blocking my view.

I run to it and clamber through a section where the stones have given up fighting the gales that beat in from the ocean. The boom of the sea is right ahead of me now, deafening.

There it is: the angry dark water of the Atlantic.

For a moment I stop, frozen by the sight of the immense power in front of me. There's a constant low growl, and mixed into it are huge pounding crashes. I swear I can almost feel the ground shaking with each beat of the ocean's unearthly drum.

The clifftop is broken, uneven, but there are wide areas of grass and a quite incredible sight: the whole side of the hill that curves down towards the hideous drop into the sea is covered in flowers. White flowers.

It doesn't seem possible. Although it's July, the weather here at the end of the world isn't summer. It's not even autumn or winter – it's no season at all, unless there's a fifth one called "storm". And yet here's a whole field of delicate white flowers, long, fluffy white flowers, blowing about in frantic waves as the wind tears in off the ocean.

Then I see her.

She's right there, in front of me, and I didn't see her at first – she's so much smaller in the landscape than I was expecting. I suddenly realise that this place is even bigger than I thought, even more powerful.

Cassie is right by the cliff edge, standing, staring out to sea. She's maybe a hundred metres away from me, and she looks as small as an ant. There are huge chasms here, the cliffs plunging down into the raging waters. Cassie is standing at the very tip of the land.

I call. I shout. I scream, but I can barely hear my own voice, so I set off and hurtle down through the white flowers, shouting as I go, "Cassie, Cassie!"

I'm almost there and she raises her arms up into the sky, as if she's welcoming something, or praying, or I don't know what.

"Cassie!" I scream for the final time, and she turns.

She doesn't seem surprised to see me. She doesn't seem ... anything. Her face is blank, her skin is almost as white as her hair, which is soaked and hanging in clumps, half blocking her eyes. Water is running down her face, and I don't know if it's rain, or ...

Then Cassie takes a step towards me, and her face crumples as she collapses into me.

We both sink to the ground, and under the pounding roar of the ocean, she sobs, silently.

We stay that way a long time.

The rain lashes at us. I'm freezing, but I don't care. My hands are raw and red. The rain has reached under my coat, under my clothes, and we both start to shiver. But still we don't move.

I lift my head and look out to sea, rain stinging my face.

The ocean is immeasurable. It moves in slow motion, the scale of it is so big. Waves roll in from far out to sea, white crests rising, rising in size, standing up as they approach the rock face below us until they are taller than high-rise buildings. Then they slam themselves against the cliff, with a boom as if a god has slapped their hand on a drum the size of the Earth.

"What were you going to do?" I say, not loud, but right into Cassie's ear so she can hear me.

She doesn't answer. Not at first.

She shifts and sits up, looks me in the face.

"I don't know," she says.

"Why did you come?" I ask.

Cassie shrugs.

"I wanted to come somewhere where I couldn't hear the hum, to drown it out. And also ... I already told you ... To get as far away as I can from everyone. Except ..."

"What?" I ask.

"I knew you'd find it. My message. I knew you'd come."

Suddenly I want to shout, but with joy. I don't feel cold any more – I feel wonderful. And I can't help smiling.

"It was clever, what you did with the letters, but you can't have known I'd go to Summit Viewpoint. You can't have known I'd find it."

Cassie shrugs again. "I believed you would."

That word. *Believe.* I look around at the world: the land, the sea – the vast energy vibrating between the two. I know what Cassie needs.

"Cassie," I say, looking her in the eyes. "I believe you. About the hum, I mean. I can't hear it, but I know it's real. It has to be."

Then she's crying and laughing at the same time.

"What do you think it means?" I ask. "Is it the Earth? Is it angry with us?"

"I don't think it knows how to be angry. I think it's trying to talk to us. Send us a message."

"Like what?"

"It's saying something like, I don't fight, I don't need to," Cassie says. "But if you try to fight me, it will be you who loses."

Far above our heads, above the storm, miles up into the air, strange electricity sparks across the atmosphere.

We stay that way a long time.

After a lifetime has passed, I pull Cassie's arm.

"Come on," I say. "Other people are worried about you too."

As we turn, Dad is there, a little way off. I can tell he's been waiting. Like us, he's soaked.

We go up to him.

"How long have you been there?" I ask. "Why didn't you come over and help?"

He smiles.

"Looked like you were doing just fine," he says. Then, "Cassie, I've got through to your parents. There's a payphone in the cafe. They'd like to speak to you."

Cassie looks blank, worried. She glances at me, at Dad.

"Go on," he says gently. "It's OK. There are some things they want to say to you."

We hurry up towards the buildings, and the rain starts to ease.

Cassie goes into the cafe and I'm about to follow, but Dad holds me back.

"Let her have some privacy, yep?" he says, and I nod.

Though we are soaked through, we sit outside on a bench, nestled against the wall of a building. Even as we sit down, a sudden ray of sunshine breaks through the clouds.

"You did well, Fitz," says Dad.

I don't know what to say. So I ignore it.

"It's weird – that field of flowers over there," I say instead.

"Where?"

I nod.

"In the long grass over there, on the cliff."

"It's not grass," says Dad. "It's called cotton grass, but it's not actually grass. It's a type of sedge."

I laugh.

"What?" says Dad.

"You should totally go on *The Chase*," I say, and then I think, *Huh, cotton.*

Cassie is taking a long time. I stand up and wander around to keep warm, and then I see something screwed into the white wall of the cafe. It's a little black notice, made of metal, with white writing on it.

CAPE WRATH
The most north-westerly point in mainland Britain. It is believed that Vikings used the cape as a navigation landmark, where they would turn their ships for home. The name "Wrath" comes from the Old Norse word "hvarf", which means "turning point".

I'm just about to call Dad over to look at the sign when Cassie comes out of the cafe. She's been crying, but when she sees me, she smiles a huge smile. I have never seen her smile before. She is so beautiful.

I don't know what to say, so I just say, "Well?"

"They're really sorry," she says. "Dad couldn't stop apologising. Mum too."

"Are they angry?"

"Not with me, no," she says. "With themselves. They say this has woken them up.

They'd got so bogged down in their work and their worry about the world that they'd forgotten about me."

"Oh," I say. "So ...? What now?"

"They've promised to try harder. They're going to see a counsellor, they said. And do stuff with me, like they used to."

"That's ... wonderful," I say. "But what about their work? Doesn't your dad think it's still too late? For the world?"

"We spoke about that too. Dad says even if the planet is going to be different from before, there's always time for *people* to change. Always. When they reach a turning point."

A turning point. And that's just so weird that I start laughing. When Cassie frowns at me, I don't say anything, I just point at the sign.

She reads it. She gets it.

She turns back to me.

"Life is really weird sometimes, isn't it?" she says.

I nod.

Dad comes over, smiling.

"Ready to turn for home?" he asks.

We nod.

"Your folks are happy for us to drive you back," Dad says to Cassie. "I've promised them you're safe, so you have to promise too. Not to do anything unsafe. Got it?"

"Got it, Mr Fitzgerald," Cassie says. "Anyway, we have things to do when we get home."

"We do?" I ask.

"Fitz," she says, grinning. "We have music to make."

Our books are tested
for children and young people by
children and young people.

Thanks to everyone who consulted on
a manuscript for their time and effort in
helping us to make our books better
for our readers.